Fun China

CHINESE ANIMALS

Written by **Alice Ma**
Illustrated by **Sheung Wong**
Reviewed by **Judith Malmsbury**

Sun Ya Publications (HK) Ltd.
www.sunya.com.hk

Charlie and Ying Ying are very good friends.
They set out on a hiking trip on a sunny day.
Suddenly, a sound in the nearby trees catches their attention.
A wise and gentle creature emerges.
It is Dragon C from China!

Charlie and Ying Ying look at each other.
They do not know it yet,
but this hike is going to be one of the best!

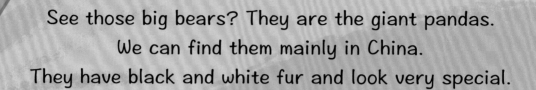

See those big bears? They are the giant pandas.
We can find them mainly in China.
They have black and white fur and look very special.

These chubby pandas are so playful.
They love to roll around and have fun.
The Chinese people love them a lot.

Look at those elf-like Tibetan antelopes.
They have a thin body and a pair of long, curved horns.

I wonder if they have ever met Santa Claus's reindeer during Christmas time.

Lean as they are,
these antelopes actually live in very cold areas.
Their fluffy layer of fur will keep them warm
even in freezing temperatures.

Are you ready to greet the Asian elephants?
They are the biggest animals in Asia.
These giants can grow as tall as a basketball hoop
and weigh as much as four buses.

Unlike their friend Jumbo the elephant
who lives in Africa, the Asian elephants
have smaller ears and a rounded back.
They used to live in China.
Now, we can find them in other countries like Thailand.

Oh, there are some monkeys!
They are called the white-headed langurs.
We can recognise them by their white head
and dark body. Their babies have an orange body.

I bet they will like the swings in the playground.

These monkeys are really good at climbing trees
and swinging from branch to branch.
It is because they have strong arms and legs.

Have you ever heard of the baiji?
It is a kind of dolphin
calling China's Yangtze River home.

Baijis are very pretty!
They have a shiny bluish-gray body
and a long, thin nose. They are so graceful
that people call them "the Goddess of the Yangtze".

Cluck-cluck.
The golden pheasants are saying hello to us.
They have a spotted tail, a bright crown
and colourful feathers. They look like
they are dressed up for a party!

14

The golden pheasants live in the forests
and mountains of China.
People all around the world
love to watch these walking rainbows.
Do you like them too?

15

In the high mountains of Asia,
there is a big, furry animal called the yak.

Yaks are strong and muscular.
They are great friends to humans
and help us carry heavy things in rocky areas.
Many Asian cultures, especially the Chinese, love yaks.

Yaks make life easier
for people living in
high mountains!
Let's give them
a round of applause!

In the high hills of China,
we can find another animal called the kiang.
It looks like a donkey but with stylish, reddish-brown hair.

Kiangs are fast runners. They enjoy running in big groups
across the beautiful mountains.
Just imagine running like the wind
and feeling the fresh air on your face.
How awesome it would be!

Hi friends, are you still with me?
Let's meet the Chinese alligators.
They dwell in the rivers and marshes of China.
They have tough skin that keeps them safe from danger.

Look up at the sky and see the beautiful crested ibises.
These birds have a red face, white-to-pink body
and black beak. They are from China
and mostly live in wetlands and forests.

But that's not all.
Do you see a special crest of feathers on its head?
It is just like a flying work of art!

This bird has a special crest. No wonder it is called the crested ibis.

The sun is setting.
It is time for Charlie and Ying Ying to go back.
They had so much fun exploring the wildlife in China.

As they say goodbye, Charlie and Ying Ying know
that they love animals much more than before.
Also, they are happy to build a friendship with Dragon C.

English - Chinese Glossary of Chinese Animals

The giant panda
- **TC** 大熊貓
- **SC** 大熊猫
- 🔊 dà xióng māo

The Tibetan antelope
- **TC** 藏羚羊
- **SC** 藏羚羊
- 🔊 zàng líng yáng

The Asian elephant
- **TC** 亞洲象
- **SC** 亚洲象
- 🔊 Yàzhōu xiàng

The white-headed langur
- **TC** 白頭葉猴
- **SC** 白头叶猴
- 🔊 bái tóu yè hóu

The baiji
- **TC** 白鰭豚
- **SC** 白鳍豚
- 🔊 bái qí tún

The golden pheasant
TC 紅腹錦雞
SC 红腹锦鸡
🔊 hóng fù jǐn jī

The kiang
TC 藏野驢
SC 藏野驴
🔊 zàng yě lú

The yak
TC 氂牛
SC 牦牛
🔊 lí niú

The Chinese alligator
TC 揚子鱷
SC 扬子鳄
🔊 yáng zǐ è

The crested ibis
TC 朱鷺
SC 朱鹭
🔊 zhū lù

27

Fun China
Chinese Animals

Author
Alice Ma

Illustrator
Sheung Wong

Reviewer
Judith Malmsbury

Executive Editor
Tracy Wong

Graphic Designer
Aspen Kwok

Publisher
Sun Ya Publications (HK) Ltd.
18/F, North Point Industrial Building, 499 King's Road, Hong Kong
Tel: (852) 2138 7998   Fax: (852) 2597 4003
Website: https://www.sunya.com.hk
E-mail: marketing@sunya.com.hk

Distributor
SUP Publishing Logistics (HK) Ltd.
16/F, Tsuen Wan Industrial Centre, 220-248 Texaco Road,
Tsuen Wan, N.T., Hong Kong
Tel: (852) 2150 2100   Fax: (852) 2407 3062
E-mail: info@suplogistics.com.hk

Printer
C & C Offset Printing Co., Ltd.
36 Ting Lai Road, Tai Po, N.T., Hong Kong

Edition
First Published in October 2023

ISBN: 978-962-08-8260-9
© 2023 Sun Ya Publications (HK) Ltd.
18/F, North Point Industrial Building, 499 King's Road, Hong Kong
Published in Hong Kong SAR, China
Printed in China